THE SECRET

A Novella Trilogy
By Kevon Halbert Sr.

I0551314

THE SECRET

Copyright 2025 KeConcepts Media LLC,"

Halbertkevon9@icloud.com

Dedication

All Glory be to God. To Tamara & Kevon Jr. for helping me to face my fears, for reading, listening, and speaking life into me and into this book when the idea was just that. Thank you to Tamara and Alisha for editing my first draft of The Secret. This book is dedicated to Shirley Halbert December 26, 1951 – December 03, 2025.

Psalm 37:4 (NIV):

"Take delight in the lord and he will give you the desires of your heart."

Chapters

Disclaimer

The characters in this book are made for entertainment purposes only. The events are false although the areas are familiar, these events never took place in the city or state the book was created in. If you or a loved one find yourself in a situation such as this call 911 or go to the nearest police station. PLEASE do not attempt anything in this book.

CHAPTER 1

Rags to Riches

The morning carried a weight Sean couldn't explain, something in his gut told him today would be different. He cruised the streets with a Joel Osteen podcast playing. His mother had told him to listen to it. Words of encouragement and breakthrough echoing louder than the engine, then it ended in prayer. Then as if the universe had spoken, he changed the channel and Rod Wave's "Rags to Riches" came on. Sean cracked a grin. Perfect timing he thought, as he sang along. The lyrics hitting harder than usual.

He couldn't help but think, he wasn't broke where he couldn't pay his bills it was the fact he couldn't afford to do much after he paid them. He had been remodeling houses for years. Pulling most of the weight on jobs, homeowners spent seven grand and he walked away with scraps. Ninety percent of the work for 10% of the pay.

The memory still burned in his mind, that's why he had started his own company. Why this job had to work out. He prayed as he turned on the client's street. "Lord let this be mine."

****
****

The House

The house wasn't much to look at, peeling paint, sagging porch. The kind of place you would call a project and mean it. Sean parked, killed the engine and grabbed his notebook.

The front door swung open before Sean had a chance to knock. A Latino male stepped out; phone to his ear, Spanish rolling smooth and quick. He ended the call when his eyes landed on Sean.

"You must be Sean;" The man said, extending his hand. "That's me." Sean said, gripping firmly as they shook hands. Carlos smiled faintly, motioning inside. "Bathrooms upstairs." He said, as Sean walked into the house closing the door behind him.

The house was empty like no one had lived in it for a while Sean thought, as he followed Carlos up the stairs. Listening as Carlos rattled off what he wanted tile, colors, fixtures. Sean took notes asking all the usual questions, trying to sound more confident than he felt. Carlos leaned against the door frame studying Sean.

"You been doing this for a while?" Carlos asked.

"About fourteen years." Sean replied.

"Good, because I want it done by the time I get back." Carlos said, looking at Sean.

"Back?" Sean said, confused. You just moved in? "He asked."

"Bought it for my girlfriend." Carlos said, simply. "First time stepping foot in it."

The two walked down the steps and to the kitchen. Carlos opened the cabinet that held a thick envelope, he handed it to Sean.

"Everything you'll need is in there." He said. "I'll call when I'm back."

Sean's fingers tightened around the envelope, Carlos shook his hand and walked out the house, just like that. Sean stood in the silence, starring at the envelope in disbelief. The envelope sat heavy in his hand. Curiosity burned, but fear gnawed at the edges of his thoughts. He slipped it into his pocket and forced himself to the truck to get his tool bag. Once upstairs, he took note that the bathroom was dated but manageable. Sean sat the tool bag down and began to pry the first piece of tub surround off the wall.

Behind it, clear plastic sheeting stretched across the studs. Strange he thought, frowning as he tore another piece down. More plastic, too neat too deliberate. His pulse picked up he ripped down another section, that's when he saw it, a package wrapped tight, hidden in layers of plastic. Sean's mouth went dry as he tugged it loose heart pounding, he tore it open just enough to peek inside. Crisp hundred- dollar bills stared back at him.

Panic

Sean staggered backwards, clutching the package. His breathe shallow, his legs weak. The bathroom seemed to be closing in on him. "This can't be real" he said, but it was. He clawed down the last panel, more plastic, more packages. Every inch of the walls stuffed. Sean knocked over his tool bag, his hands trembled.

Every sound became deafening. The crack of the floorboard, the hum of traffic outside, the rasp of his own breath. He bolted for the stairs envelope still jammed in his pocket. The front door, he yanked on it. Locked. His chest seized, Sean peeked out the blind. No one, he ran to the back door. Empty yard. Sean swallowed hard, forcing himself back upstairs.

A contractor bag lay half rolled up on the floor. Black, thick perfect he thought as his hands moved faster than his brain, loading the bag until it bulged like Santa's in the movies.

"This is a blessing," Sean told himself. Deep down he knew blessings didn't come wrapped in plastic stuffed behind a wall and nothing that easy came without a price.

****
****

CHAPTER 2

Temptation

Sean came home, he was pacing the floor. Grinning then a frown; the thoughts we're coming like downloads from a computer. Kish watched the back and forth as Sean was laughing.

He only stopped when Kish asked, "Bae, why you all happy? What's going on?" It was at that moment Sean noticed Kish standing there.

"Bae," Sean said looking nervously at Kish. "I gotta tell you something, but you have to promise not to tell anybody."

"You're making me nervous," Kish said as Sean grabbed Kish's hands.

"I went to meet this guy for a job remodeling his bathroom." Kish began to speak as Sean shook his head no. Sean pulls the envelope out of his pocket. "He gave me this," Sean gave Kish the envelope. "I started to work on the bathroom tearing down the tub surround and found a lot of money in the walls."

"Who's, money, was it?" Kish asked. Sean looked confused.

"That's the thing, the guy that bought the house never stepped foot in it until now." He said.

"I saw something like this on tv, you have to turn it in and if no one claims it it's yours." Kish said. Sean shook his head no.

"This is a blessing" he said. "I just can't hand it over and hope we see it again." Sean said.

"How much is it?" Kish asked. Kish was in deep thought, when Sean came back inside with the bags of money.

"We gone have to leave town" she said, as Sean opened the bags up. "Someone will be looking for that money." Kish said.

"How can we ride around with this. Plus, I have to finish the job like nothing ever happened." Sean said. "By the time he comes back I will be done and there will be no need for me to be around when who's ever money it is comes looking for it." Sean said. Sean goes to one of the bags and grabs money out. "This is one hundred- thousand take it." He said.

Kish took the money with a look of surprise and the biggest grin.

"We need to invest maybe in a store or property just in case anything happens." Sean said. "I have to meet Light Skin Chris at the bar, then I'm going to count and hide the money. I will be back sometime tomorrow." He said.

"Sean be careful Kish said, and don't tell Chris nothing you don't want nobody to know."

Kish looks at the money stands up and places her hands on Sean's face. "I love you" she said, this money ain't worth losing you. If this is the plan, you have to be smart." She said. Sean kisses Kish on the lips grabs the bags of money and walks out the door.

****
****

_____

The Club

Sean had thought long and hard about what Kish was saying, and she was right. He couldn't tell Chris shit. Chris was loyal, his best friend since grade school. But being wild and attention seeking was his flaw. He wanted to be in the streets bad, but he had big dreams just like everyone else. He just didn't want to work a 9 to 5. Sean couldn't blame him; it was Sean's dream to be able to do whatever his heart desired. Chris was going to get his shot. Sean just hoped it didn't back fire.

****
****

After he counted the money, minus the hundred- thousand he had given Kish, it was six million nine hundred- thousand dollars.

He had loaded it all up in the closet and closed the doors. He pulled up to a packed parking lot which wasn't surprising considering it was a Friday night. After squeezing into a parking spot, he hopped out the truck and headed inside. He knew Chris would be at the bar.

They called him Light Skin Chris because he tried to bleach his skin to look like Micheal Jackson when they were kids and ended up in the hospital for a week with skin burn. It was their way of teasing him without people knowing what he had done.

Sean walked into the club and immediately saw Chris. He was the loudest thing at the bar, that laugh was irritating, but distinctive. Next to him was a bald dude that had three other guys around him. Chris looked back saw Sean and yelled "That's my dawg!" It seemed like everyone in the club looked to see who he was talking about.

The bald guy said "You do all kinds of work on houses huh? Yo man tryna link, maybe in exchange you could renovate a couple houses for me."

"I wouldn't usually turn it down, but my plate is full right now," Sean said grabbing Chris by the arm. "Can I talk to you in private?" he asked. Chris stood up and walked to a corner of the bar. Sean gave him the envelope "Call me so we can talk" Sean said, and walked out the club.

****
****

Tony Keys

Tony Keys dials a number outside the gas station.

"Hello," a man's voice answered. Keys spoke in a low deep voice. "I'm out," Keys said.

"Boss, where you at?" The man asked. "Gas station downtown E. 9th." Keys said.

"Stay put we on our way, the man responded and Boss we found that problem you were, looking for."

"Is it fixed?" Keys asked. "A little too good, the man answered, it won't break again."

Keys hung up the phone.

****
****

Sean couldn't help but think he dodged a bullet, as he climbed in the truck. Whatever Chris had going on he didn't want to be a part of it. Still, some how he felt that he would end up in debt also. Finish the job was all that was on his mind. He headed back to Carlos' house, there was a lot of work to be done.

Money was the biggest motivation. He hadn't changed clothes, slept or ate much and on que, a Rally's was open on Broadway Ave. As he pulled up, he ordered a Big Buford combo, with a Coke. Slowly pulling to the next window he thought about investing. He opened his phone and began looking up houses, condo's, storefronts and anything that was available. In case he had to give the money back he wouldn't be broke.

After getting the food he drove back to the house, ate and went back to work. It would take the rest of the day to demo and prep for the remodel.

****
****

"Boss, it's morning should we ride past the house see if it's empty, one of Keys men asked?"

"No." Keys said, "Just wait I'm fresh out. The FEDs could still be watching me.

Carlos is the only person that knew about that ledger, with him gone I know it's safe."

With a look of surprise the man asked, "How can you be so sure he didn't find it?" the man asked.

"I wound be dead for creating it and he would have a key to the city, instead of his brains blown out on the sidewalk." Keys said, "Now let's celebrate."

****
****

The Salon

Kish walked into the salon, "What's up?" Kish asked. "Girl I'm so glad you could squeeze me in." Kish said.

The stylist smiled and said, "Sis we family." As a Latino woman stood up from the chair. "Kish, this my Dominican friend, Alana Cruz" the stylist said. "She tryna sell her house, her boyfriend was killed the other day."

Kish put her hand to her mouth. "I'm so sorry to hear that" Kish said. "This can only be fate because I've been looking to buy some property. Where is it at and how much do you want for it?" Alana's mood changed.

"E. 84th." She said, with a heavy Spanish accent. "All I want is twenty-five thousand." Alana said.

"Girl that's a steal!" the stylist responded, "but I don't have time to fix it up and rent it out, that's too much."

Kish touched Alana's hand and said, "I will give you cash if you let me get my hair done first," as she sat in the chair.

"See Alana girl the stylist said, you just gotta have faith it's all gone work out. Gods plan is always better than our own." said the stylist.

****
****

The Company You Keep

Keys answers the phone as they walk up to the bar inside the club. "Hello, what? Tonight?" he asked. He grabs a napkin writes down something, and places it in his pocket and hangs up the phone. He signals to his men to leave and heads to the door.

Sean walks into the club right past Keys and his crew. He pulls out a hundred- dollar bill, places it on the bar and asks the bartender for a Remedy. It was Remy Martin, Simply Limeade juice, stirred with ice.

"Light Skin Chris been in here tonight, Tosha?" Sean asked.

"Not yet." Tosha replied, "but he should watch the company he keeps."

Sean frowned, "What happened?" he asked.

Tosha looked back at the other bartender behind her "Virgil I'm going on break. Sean, meet me at the table in the corner," she said.

Sean grabbed his drink, went to the table and sat down. Tosha grabbed the mini fan, went to the table lit her Black & Mild then sat down.

"Look." she said, bluntly. "I saw y'all talking to Shaq the other day. He is bad news and I don't know how they boss got out of jail. You literally just walked past all of them." She said.

Sean was confused. "How is Chris involved?" he asked Tosha.

Shaking her head no, she looked at Sean and said "Whatever was in that envelope you gave him, he gave it to Shaq. Shaq gone push the limit and if Chris don't have the money, he gone disappear suddenly." As Tosha spoke, every word hit like a baseball bat to the gut.

If Chris gave Shaq the money he was going to expect more and somehow, they were both going to end up in debt. He thanked Tosha with a hundred-dollar bill and a hug as he walked out of the club to the truck.

****
****

The Surprise

He called Chris, of course no answer. He drove home fast as he could, he hadn't seen Kish in some time. It was normal her being a nurse who worked twelve- hour shifts. They wouldn't see each other for days.

His gut was giving him an uneasy feeling. It was hard to tell if it was Chris, or did Kish run for mayor with the money, he had given her. He pulled up in the driveway and let out a sigh of relief, grabbed his things and headed for the door. As soon as he opened it.

He saw Kish coming to greet him, drink in hand.

"Bae, you won't believe what happened today." Kish said, with a faint slur.

"What?" Sean replied, not knowing if he wanted the answer.

"I went to get my hair and nails done." Kish said, holding her nails out so Sean could see, "and my stylist introduced me to a lady selling a house. Guess how much though?" Kish said excitedly.

"A hundred- thousand." Sean said, sarcastically.

"No. Twenty- five thousand, Kish said, excited. "When she saw I had cash she burst out in tears." Kish said. "Her boyfriend was killed. It was sad. So, let's eat, make love and then we can go see it together tomorrow."

****
****

The House

"Boss. I know you said, lay off the house. We just rode past it. No movement it still looks empty," said one of the goons.

Keys shook his head. "Good." he said.

"Tomorrow around noon go get the ledger. It's in the living room ceiling you can't miss the patch and once you have it, unalive anyone in the house." Keys said.

"I'm on it boss the man said. Oh, I have something for you," The man said. As he opened the door and in walks ten beautiful women all shapes, sizes and scantily dressed.

The other men were excited as the women began to mingle.

****
****

As they locked up the house and hopped in the car, Sean had already imagined about ten different houses and what it could look like. He reclined his seat and closed his, eyes. When he awoke, he thought it was a joke, it was the house he had found the money in.

Instantly he began to sweat, he could hear his heart pounding. Kish was inside the house with the front door open, before he could get a word out. He got out of the truck and went inside.

"Who did you say you got this house from?" he asked, nervously while looking around.

"Alana Cruz, Kish said. Her boyfriend bought it for her, but he was killed a couple days ago."

Sean grabbed his head. "Carlos is dead he mumbled. The money."
He said, as he began to run up the stairs to the bathroom. He
sighed with relief. "It's still intact" he said. As Kish came up the
stairs behind him.

"What's wrong?" Kish asked. Nervously?

Sean looked around then whispered, "This is the house."

"I know I bought it," Kish said sarcastically.

"No, this is the house I found the money in," Sean said.

Knock, knock, knock. "Police" a man's voice yelled from the
door. Then the doorbell rang. Kish looked at Sean.

"Don't look all crazy now, Sean said. This yo house."

"One second, Kish yelled, from the steps. What am I supposed to
do?" She asked, nervously.

"Tell them you just bought the house." Sean nudged Kish toward
the steps as he stood there listening.

"How can I help you officers?" Kish asked.

"Detective Shambone." He replied, "this is detective Ponder and I
am Detective Joe Shambone. You wouldn't happen to be Ms.
Cruz by chance, would you?" he asked.

"No." Kish said. "I just purchased the house from Ms. Cruz, I was
just checking it out. Is there a problem?" Kish asked.

"No, ma'am." Det. Shambone said, quickly. "Would you happen
to have a number for Ms. Cruz?" he asked.

"No, I'm sorry we met through a mutual friend, she was leaving
to go back home." Kish responded.

"Dominican Republic?" Det. Shambone asked

"Yes." Kish replied. "Is this about her boyfriend?"

That question raised Detective Shambone's curiosity. "Did you know Mr. Ortiz?" he Asked.

"No." Kish replied. "She had mentioned that he was killed and that's why she was selling then leaving."

Detective Shambone looks around and saw the decal on the truck same as the cards found on Carlos Ortiz. He looks at Lilly then asked Kish, "Are you here alone?"

"No." she answered, "I'm here with my fiancée." "Sean!" She yelled.

Sean came down the stairs nervously looks at the detectives. "Yeah Bae? What's going on?" he asked.

"Do you know Carlos Ortiz?" Det. Shambone asked.

"Yes. Well not personally, but I've done some work for him," Sean replied.

"What about Ms. Cruz?" Det. Shambone asked.

"No. Only my fiancée met her." Sean replied.

"Well, I won't keep you two any longer," Det. Shambone said. reaching into his pocket. "If you two remember anything that might help this investigation don't hesitate to give us a call." He handed Kish then Sean a card as he and Detective Ponder headed to their unmarked car.

"What made him ask about me?" Sean asked.

"I don't know," Kish responded. "He looked at the truck and asked, calm down." She said, "if we were in trouble we'd be in handcuffs."

Nah, Sean shook his head no. "He knew the answers to those questions before he asked. Come get your gun out the truck" Sean said. "I gotta see what's up with Chris."

****
****

CHAPTER 3

Detective Joe Shambone

Phone rings once, twice, three times. "Hello, Shambone here," the Detective answered half asleep from his bed. "Hold on, let me get my pen," he said. "Corner of 88th & Garfield Blvd" he repeated then hung up the phone. "So much for a quiet two weeks," he says to himself as he gets up to get dressed.

Detective Shambone pulls up, turns the car off and gets out.

"Lilly what do we have here?" he asked.

"Deceased male, 36-year-old Latino. Carlos Ortiz, gunshot wound to the head. We are currently interviewing witnesses, there is also a camera across the street. We are waiting on word if they have anything," Lilly reported.

"Run him, see if he has a record." Det. Shambone said.

"Wherever he works, any known ties, whatever you can get me. He pissed somebody off that didn't mind killing him." Det. Shambone said.

"I'm on it." Det. Lilly Ponder responded. "Sorry you don't get to retire in peace," she said.

****
****

As Det. Shambone sat at his desk Lilly walks into the room.

"Do you remember the Keys case?" Lilly asks.

"Refresh my memory," Det. Shambone replied.

"About six years ago we arrested Tony Keys," Lilly started. "We had him in our cross hairs for a double murder of the Cortez brothers."

Shambone sat up in his chair. "I remember that," he said. "The FEDS took the case."

"Right." Lilly responded. "Well Carlos Ortiz was the federal informant in that case with Keys. I called Federal and was told that Keys for unspecified reasons had been in solitary confinement for the past five years. Guess when he got out?" Lilly asked.

"Yesterday," Det. Shambone answered.

"We're going to miss you Detective," Lilly responded.

"Lilly does Vanessa still work for Keller Morgan Real Estate?" Shambone asked.

"You know she does" Lilly responded. "She would love to do you a favor, but you have to get the information yourself," Lilly said.

"I know take one for the team." Det Shambone replied. "I need to know of any property that has been purchased. Houses, warehouses, condos, anything she can get me." Detective Shambone said.

"I'm on it Detective," Lilly replied.

****
****

The Law

Det. Shambone knocks on the door as the sun began to set. Vanessa opens the door with a robe on and a glass of wine in hand.

Det. Shambone takes one look and says, "Old habits die hard, huh Vanessa?" Det. Shambone said with a grin on his face.

"I got something that needs to be killed," Vanessa said sarcastically, but meaning every word.

"Now look I refuse to be treated like a rack of ribs out here for some information. You do know I'm the law?" Det. Shambone said with a serious face.

Vanessa had a look of shock on her face. "I don't eat ribs Detective, I eat glizzies, she said.

"Glizzies, what's that?" the Detective asked confused.

"Polish boys, beef franks, you if you quit playing," she said.

Det Shambone chuckled. "You do know this is an active murder case and withholding information can get you 15 to 20?" he said.

As he pulled out his handcuffs and slowly walks into the house towards Vanessa. He turns Vanessa around placing her hands on the wall and closes the door.

****
****

Det. Shambone walk into the investigation room and goes to the board. Staring at the picture of Carlos Ortiz's dead body.

He turns to Lilly and says, "Fill me in as I go. Carlos Ortiz shot dead execution style last know associate Tony Keys. Gun runner, drug dealer, murderer. Released same day as murder, but not a suspect in the shooting. What was found at the scene?" Det Shambone asked.

"Business cards to a construction company" Lilly reports. "Personal possessions were still in the victim's pocket, $1200.00 cash and a cell phone she rattled off."

"What's the name of the business on the cards?" Det Shambone asks.

"2K'S Construction LLC, it says Sean Flattery," Lilly responded.

"Get me an address on Flattery, our source said Ortiz bought a house cash for one, Alana Cruz. 26yo, female from Dominican Republic. We find her maybe she can point us in the right direction," Det Shambone says.

"Let's see if we can find where Keys is hanging out, he likes high end clubs, women and lots of them. He will have an entourage so, we split up. If you see him just observe and

report back to me," Det. Shambone orders. Lilly walks over to Det. Shambone.

"They didn't see much on the cameras," she said. "No witnesses with hard evidence either."

"If Keys is behind this." Det. Shambone says it's about money or what Ortiz knew that got him killed. Check in if you see something, if not see you tomorrow and be safe," Det. Shambone says.

Lilly responds, "You too Detective, sure you don't want me to come with?" she asks.

"I'll be fine, long night for me." Det Shambone said. "Oh, and Lilly 4999 East 84th check in the system and meet me there tomorrow at 10'oclock sharp," says Det Shambone. "Ok Detective," Lilly replies as she writes it in her

notebook.

****
****

Det. Shambone entered the club. He scanned the bar, no sign of Tony Keys or his entourage. He noticed Tosha talking to a younger gentleman in the corner. Det. Shambone nods toward the bar, then grabs a seat. A moment later, Tosha walks behind the bar and grabs the Hennessey.

"You know if people knew my uncle was twelve, I'd be up shits creek." Tosha said, placing the shot of Hennessey in front of her uncle.

Det. Shambone smiled, swirling the drink in his glass before responding. "How's your mother doing Tosha?" he asked. "She cool, need a man." Tosha replied.

Shambone laughed, "You know she can't stand nobody but you." he responded.

"She heard you were retiring. She was happy you made it out in one piece." Tosha said.

 Det. Shambone looked around and then asked, "You seen Tony Keys around lately?"

"It's funny you asked, he just left 15 to 20 minutes before you walked in. Please tell me that's not your last case before retirement?" Tosha asked.

Det. Shambone looked at his watch, then at Tosha. "Every minute that goes by its looking more and more like it." He said. "Give me a call if something goes down, be safe and tell Sandra, I said hi," he said, as he prepared to get up and leave the club.

****
****

The House Continued

Kish grabbed her gun out of the truck and kissed Sean, then she went in the house closing the door behind her.

Sean grabs his phone to call Chris as soon as he gets in the truck, but in frustration puts it back down on the center console.

"His ass better be there!" He says, as he puts the truck in reverse to leave.

****
****

CHAPTER 4

No Turning Back

Shaq, lil-A, and Bam are in the car.

"Turn right here. When you get to the stop sign keep straight. I'll tell you when to stop." Shaq directed from the passenger seat.

"How we gone get in? Kick the door or something?" Lil-A asked.

"I don't know." Shaq responded. "Shit if its empty I might have you climb through the window or something." Shaq said.

"I'd rather climb through a window then walk through a door." Bam replied.

"Just check the doors" Shaq responded to him with irritation laced in his words.

"It's empty we rode past here a couple days ago, and nobody was there." Bam said.

"Go straight to the living room, Keys said there is a patch in the ceiling. Bust it open, get the book and leave. This the house right here." Shaq said, pointing to the house.

Lil-A pulled up across the street from the house and grabbed the baseball bat from the back seat.

"Turn around and park by the tree" Bam said, pointing toward the tree.

"Man, we gone need a ladder or something," Lil-A said.

"Nigga you Bob the builder," Shaq asked. "Get the shop vac out the trunk and get up all the dust and debris too. Get yo ass out." Shaq said.

Lil-A and Bam walked up to the door looking very suspicious. Bam checked the door handle, surprisingly it was unlocked. They walked in and closed the door.

Kish was in the attic unaware of the men, when she heard a thud, then another. She came down the attic steps. The sound grew louder as she walked out the bedroom, into the hallway and down the living room stairs.

"That's it, I can see it," Lil-A said to Bam. The men were knocking a hole in the ceiling when Kish stopped at the landing.

Gun pointed at Lil-A she yelled, "Don't move."

"This Bitch got a gun," Lil-A said shocked.

"She ain't gone shoot shit," Bam replied brazenly walking towards Kish.

She fired two shots hitting Bam. Lil-A tried to run for the door, as Kish fired two more shots. Now, both men lay on the floor motionless. As Kish dropped the gun, tears running down her face. She grabbed her phone and called Sean.

Shaq heard the gunshots and quickly hopped in the driver's seat looking at the house. He waited for a second then pulled off.

****
****

Come On Man

Sean pulled up to Light Skin Chris's house. He got out of the truck in hurry leaving his phone behind. As he knocked on the door it creaked open. Sean pushed it open the rest of the way. Only to see boxes everywhere and Light Skin Chris oblivious to Sean starring at him.

Chris looked up, saw Sean and with a grin smiled and said, "I was about to call you back, but my phone been jumping with plays," he said.

"What's with all the boxes? You moving?" Sean asked.

"Close that door real quick." Chris replied, looking past Sean to make sure no one was around.

Sean closes the door and asks, "What's going on Chris and what's that smell?"

Chris jumps up happily. "Weed," he says "a hundred pounds to be exact."

Sean open's one of the boxes to find it full of zip locked bags of weed.

"You gotta be shitting me," Sean said shaking his head. "You don't have to do this and how did you get so much?" He asked.

"Shaq." Chris said "The dude from the bar. I gave him the envelope you gave me and he plugged me. We good for it." Chris said.

"We," Sean replied. "I know you ain't put my name in it," he said.

"We sell it, give Shaq his money and we cool." Chris said. "I did the math a hundred pounds at $2,000 a piece that's two hundred thou-wow. Shaq only get half of that. Plus, I figured you could stop doing them odd jobs like Holmes on Holmes." Chris said.

"I gotta go," Sean said. "Try not to go to jail."

Sean walked out of Chris' house with a headache. He wasn't mad, Chris was only trying to help. Chris didn't know about the money. With 200 grand worth of marijuana in their possession and yes, their because Sean would bet that his ass was on the line just as much as Chris'.

Sean's life before finding this money didn't seem so bad now. As he opened the door to get into the truck, he saw his phone and then saw the missed calls from Kish. He listened to the voicemails. She was talking a mile a minute. All he could hear was book and two dead. He dropped the phone and headed to Carlos' house, well Kish house. It didn't matter he was on his way.

Sean pulled up on the street and saw police cars, ambulances, even the coroner on the scene. He hopped out the truck and ran to the house before police could stop him. Kish ran up to Sean, as he went under the caution tape. Sean hugged her as tight as he could while watching Detectives Shambone and Ponder walk over toward them.

****
****

"Mr. Flattery" Det. Shambone said. "This can't be a coincidence; this is the second time today. You sure there is nothing you failed to mention? Now, would be a great time." Det. Shambone asked locking eyes with Sean.

Sean grabbed Kish and asks, "Are you ok? What happened?" Kish looked at Sean and hugs him, crying harder.

"Do you have any idea what they were looking for?" Det. Ponder asked. "There's a big hole in the ceiling. It just seems odd for a random break in," she said.

"We told you, we just walked into the house when you two showed up," Sean said. "I left shortly after y'all and they must've come right after that," he explained.

 Kish holding back tears mumbled, "I didn't even know they were in the house," she cried.

"You came down the stairs see the perps then what?" Det. Shambone asked.

"I said don't move." Kish gestured as if she still held the gun. "One guy said, she ain't gone shoot shit and came toward me, I shot him twice. Then the other one rushed toward me and I shot him too," she said.

"Did they find something in the ceiling?" Lilly asked waiting for an answer.

"I just saw the bat and debris on the floor. It happened so quick I didn't have time to look," she said trembling.

"Do you have somewhere safe to go for a while?" Det. Shambone asked. "We will need both of you all's contact information." He said.

****
****

You Did What

After giving all the necessary information, they left the house. Sean looked at Kish and asked, "Didn't you say something about a book on my voicemail?"

Kish sat up straight like she had been struck by lightning. "OH SNAP!" She said. "The first guy I shot had this in his hand." She said as she reached into her purse.

"What is it?" Sean asked.

"A journal or something," Kish said. "It has names, addresses, and dates. I saw it and panicked so, I called you then the police," she said.

"We have millions and now someone's book with every killing and corrupt person we could think of in it." Sean said slamming his hand on the steering wheel.

"What do you think we should do call the detectives?" Kish asked.

"And get killed, cause they on the take and think we know something." Sean said shaking his head no.

"If I had known that was the house the money came from, I wouldn't have bought it." Kish said, apologetically.

Sean inhaled deeply then exhaled slowly. "I know Bae," he said as they rode in silence.

****
****

CHAPTER 5

I Might Need Security

They pulled into the Embassy Suites parking lot. It was far enough away from

everything, plus a continental breakfast and a bar. Sean needed a drink. He

wondered if they made Remedy's as he nervously scanned the parking lot making

sure, they weren't followed. The hotel doors slid open as they walked in, the clerk at

the front desk greeted them with a smile. "Welcome to the Embassy Suites, will the

two of you be checking in?" The clerk asked. "Yes." Sean answered. "Do you have a

king suite that overlooks the parking lot?" He asked. "Let me see." The clerk said,

typing in the computer.

"Looks like we can accommodate your request. I would just need a debit or credit

card, along with a valid ID." "Ok your all set, take the elevator to 5 get off and take a left your room will be the third door on the left. Enjoy your stay. Press 5 on the phone in your suite to call the front desk if you need assistance." The clerk informed them.

Sean, thanked the clerk and headed toward the elevators. "Maybe we can move to Puerto Rico." Kish said.

Sean laughed. "We don't even know who's looking for us." she said. "It could be anybody we walk past."

Sean shook his head. "I know, they were in the house and didn't Know you where there. So, that means they were looking for that book not us." Sean Said reassuring her.

"I killed two people." Kish said, her voice cracking as tears began to run down her face.

"Bae they might not know who we are or that we have the money and book." Sean said holding her close.

"They have a book full of people helping them. How can we out think all of them?" Kish asked.

"I think I might know somebody who can help." Sean answered.

****
****

Shaq walks into the room where Keys is waiting. "Boss, I have real bad news." Shaq said.

"Spit it out." Keys replied.

"Somebody killed Lil-A and Bam." Shaq said, nervously.

"Somebody?" Keys asked.

"We went to the house Lil-A and Bam went in. Couple minutes later I heard gunshots. I waited till I heard sirens then pulled off. Lil-A and Bam never came out." Shaq said.

"Who got the ledger?" Keys asked.

"Boss." Shaq said, shaking his head. "I don't know if they found it, or if the police have it, or nothing." Shaq confessed.

"Find out who got my shit, and who this somebody is." Keys said irritated.

****
****

Sean was hanging up the phone when Chris called. He wasn't sure if he wanted to talk to him, but he answered it anyway.

"Hello," Sean answered hesitantly.

"Man, I need yo help," Chris replied, shamefully.

 "What you done did now?" Sean asked, placing his hand on his head to prevent the headache.

"I didn't do nothing." Chris responded quickly. "These grimy ass females!" Chris shouted. "I had some bad bitches come through. I knew I shouldn't have trusted them, they slipped something in the weed we was smoking. I woke up with my dick in a pan of peach cobbler, and like 50 pounds missing. Man, Shaq gone kill me." Chris explained.

"Man, just meet me at the Embassy Suites in a couple hours." Sean said, texting Chris the room number. "Don't tell nobody, don't call nobody. Come straight here.

" Sean said and hung up the phone. "I need a miracle," Sean said. Taking off his clothes and turning on the shower... Sean came out too food Kish had delivered. Finally, they ate in peace making fun of each other and the situation. Before they knew it two hours had almost passed. They were finally relaxed, as they began to kiss someone knocked at the door.

<u>OOG</u>

"What up?" Sean said, as he opened the door. "I ain't seen yo ass in years,"

OOG said, smiling. "What you been up to?" OOG asked. "Staying out the way." Sean replied.

"I don't want know smoke either." OOG replied. I just want to make this money and make love to my beautiful wife" he said, stepping into the room as Sean motioned for the two to come in.

"Wife. You married now?" Sean said.

"Yeah man, this my wife Desirae. Met her on the set of "All This Meat."

"Y'all do porn?" Sean asked.

"Naw Man!" OOG responded. "It's a show like survivor, but for vegans." OOG clarified.

"Oh ok," Sean said.

"You have to survive in the woods for thirty days and the couple that makes it without eating meat wins." OOG said.

"Y'all won?" Sean asked.

"Almost," OOG responded. "Came down to us and another couple. One day left, this dirty motherfucka gone come to our tent with a rabbit cooked to perfection. I still don't know where he got that seasoned salt and Sweet Baby's from. We were still eating when the helicopter landed to take us home." OOG said.

"Damn. So, what you doing now?" Sean asked.

"Acting," OOG said, producer recognized me from the show asked me to audition for a part. I been doing movies and commercials ever since." OOG said.

"You were the biggest, toughest, dude on our street," Sean said. "That's kind of why I called you."

Sean was about to explain everything when there was a knock at the door.

Sean opened it to see Chris looking pathetic. "Come on in," Sean said. Closing the door behind him as he entered. Then proceeded to tell everyone what happened.

"So, let's get this straight," Chris said. "You found millions and ain't tell me shit. You know the fucked-up part, them was Shaq's boys Kish shot. So, that has to be Tony Keys' ledger they looking for." Chris said.

"Tony Keys?" Sean asked.

"Gun runner, drug dealer, cold hearted killer. All around bad news." Chris said, dramatically. "I heard he got out and that explains why, Shaq gave me all that weed." Chris said.

"Explain it to us then." Sean said.

"Keys does work for people all over the city. Stuff you couldn't imagine, so he keeps a ledger that way no one can throw him to the wolves. Without that book he a steak sandwich. He gone kill y'all when he finds you. Unless you give the ledger back." Chris said.

"Damn." Sean said.

"If the house is in your name, they probably already know who you are." Desirae added.

"OH SHIT! I can't get killed. I'm calling the Detectives." Kish said, frantically reaching for her phone.

"Wait." Sean said. "Chris knows one of Keys men. When you go to pay him for the weed just give him the book back. Make it look like he the man, that got it back. OOG can go so they don't suspect a thing." Sean said.

"Seriously! Give it back?"

OOG asked. "All we want is the money Sean said, and far as we know, no one is looking for that. Sean replied. "But, how do we do that?" Kish asked.

"Let me handle that," OOG said.

"Chris, you give it back. Sean said, OOG will be the guy who found it…"

✳✳
✳✳

The Plan

Chris listens as Double OOG starts going over what he will say.

"The contents of this bag should take care of any debt or ill will against those who found said contents." OOG rehearsed.

"Who you about to speak to Dr. Umar?" Chris asked.

"That Denzel shit gone get you killed, if something goes down you on yo own." Chris said.

"Most gangsters want things to go smooth as possible. OOG said. "I'm a new face so, they'll probably follow us once they get the money and ledger. I told Desirae to get a room on the other side of the hotel." OOG said.

"Tony Keys don't play; they follow us back to the hotel then what?" Chris asked.

"Then we know they looking for Sean and Kish. So, we make a plan B." OOG said, as he pulls out his phone and begins taking pictures of every page in the book.

"We take the pictures to who the police?" Chris sked.

"That's one idea or we use them as leverage." OOG replied.

"They can't kill us because they don't know who has copies." Chris replied. "This the spot right here." Chris said, "just let me do the talking." Chris double checks the book bag as they both exit the car.

OOG follows Chris into the club. Tosha is the first to notice the two enter the bar. Shaq asked, "Chris what up? I see you got some security."

"He cool, that's my dude, he just too gangsta. Check this out." Chris said, giving Shaq the bookbag. "I brought something for you. My guy threw in a piece offering also." Chris said.

Shaq grabbed the bag, looked inside and whispered something to one of his men.

"You made all this in less than 48 hours? Shit, I need to be working with you." Shaq said, sarcastically looking at his men. "So, who do I owe the favor too?" Shaq asked.

"They call me OOG." He said, "let's just say the parties involved acted in self-defense, but after being made aware of the error this is an attempt to rectify the situation."

"Damn," Shaq said. "Can't argue with that… Is it all here?" He asked. "Every penny," Chris replied. "We good?" Chris asked.

"We good." Shaq answered, as he shakes Chris's hand then OOG's.

Shaq turned to his guy and whisper's, "Follow them nigga's let me know where they go."

Then walked off.

****
****

CHAPTER 6

Connecting The Dots

Detective Shambone answers the phone. "Wait- wait slow down," he says. Does anyone have a weapon… a bookbag? Flattery the contractor? He gave it to one of Keys' men? Just stay calm and keep an eye out," Det. Shambone said hanging up.

"Detective." Lilly said. "How does Flattery fit into this?" she asked.

"I don't know. "Det. Shambone said as he places Flattery's business card on the board. "The only connection so far, is that house. Something that came from it or still inside of it is getting people killed. We need to check it again maybe we missed something," he said as he headed out the room.

****
****

Shaq walks into the room where Keys is sitting at the table.

"Where you been?" Keys asked. "I've been calling you for about an hour," he said irritated.

"Turns out my man's knew I rolled with you and did me a solid," Shaq said. "I figure since I'm saving yo ass you owe me one," he said cockily sliding the ledger across the table.

"How he get this?" Keys asked looking through the ledger then up at Shaq.

"From whoever unalived Lil-A and Bam," Shaq responded.

"When they found out who they worked for they came to me as a peace offering." Shaq explained.

"Peace huh, you find out who was in that house?" Keys asked.

"I'm already on it." Shaq replied. "But let me ask you this you got what you wanted, you gone bring more heat by going after whoever killed Lil-A and Bam?" Shaq asked.

"Fuck Lil-A and Bam they ass was some human shields," Keys said. "Besides it's enough dirt in this ledger to bury everyone in it, including me. So, ask yourself this if you were in my shoes, would you get buried or do the burying?" Keys asked.

"I guess foolish living will send you to an early grave," Shaq said. "Vel and Keshaun following the lead on who killed Lil-A and Bam. So, we have time to kick back," he said.

✳✳
✳✳

<u>One Shot</u>

Detective Shambone walked into the club, scans the room and spots Tosha serving drinks at the bar.

"It's crowded." Det. Shambone said aloud as he sat at the bar.

Tosha came over and asked "The usual unc?"

"Still working." He replied, "Just give me a ginger ale with ice," he said pulling out a ten- dollar bill and placing it on the bar.

Tosha grabbed a glass rinsed it then filled it with ice. She gave her uncle the glass and ginger ale can. She froze with shock and fear as Tony Keys walks in with Shaq. Tosha taps her uncle's hand as the two men sat at the bar waiving for the other barmaid to serve them.

Tosha looks at her uncle, who gives her a nod to go take their order.

"Go head Jenny I got this." Tosha said, to the other barmaid.

"What can I get you two?" Tosha asked, Keys and Shaq.

"I've been gone a while what's the house special?" Keys asked.

"Remedy's," Tosha replied. "It's Remy Martin and Simply Limeade juice stirred with ice. I like it better with Cosamigos Reposado though." Tosha replied.

"Let me get one of them with Cosamigos." Keys said.

"Make it two." Shaq yelled out holding up two fingers.

Tosha looked at her uncle nervously as she began to make their drinks.

Detective Shambone, yet to be noticed by Keys or Shaq looked at his phone to see the time 5:27pm. As he looked up from his phone in walks Lilly with an envelope. She walks over to Keys and places it on the bar as Tosha was serving the men their drinks.

Det. Shambone shrank in his seat, his left-hand covering half of his face. He continued to watch Lilly interact with Keys unable to hear over the loud music and chatter. He watched her every move.

Would Lilly try and take down Keys? Then again, she had the envelope as if she knew he was here all along, he thought. A few moments later Lilly walked out the club still unaware Det. Shambone had witnessed the whole transaction.

Keys ordered another drink and downed it like water. He said something to Shaq, stood up and walked out the club.

Det. Shambone waited a second, then placed a ten-dollar bill on the bar and followed Keys. When Det. Shambone came out of the club Keys was starting his RAM 1500. It was hard to get a color, it was night time and the parking lot to the club was dimly lit. It looked black or maybe green.

As Keys pulled out of the parking spot Det. Shambone climbed in his unmarked car and proceeded to follow Keys. Side streets seemed to be his path of choice. Eventually they came to the intersection of Turney & McCracken. As they continued down McCracken lights from the train tracks began to flash. Keys crossed first as the gate came down.

Det. Shambone hit the gas. If he lost Keys, he may not get another shot.

It was too late. The train sped past as Keys' brake lights could only be seen in the distance. As the train horn blew Detective Shambone knew he had missed an opportunity.

There were so many questions that needed answers. He had a feeling that he should keep things hush until, he was sure.

****
****

Make it Make Sense

Shaq's phone rings. As he removes it from his pocket, he sees that it's Vel and Keshaun. "What's the word?" Shaq answers.

"They just pulled up at the Embassy Suites." Vel replied.

"Follow them. I need to know who's in that hotel room." Shaq said.

"I'm on it, but what if it's just them two?" Vel asked. "Then they found the book in a dead man's hands," Shaq said angrily.

"You, my dawg, but if they gave you what you wanted. Why we on they ass?" Vel replied.

"I gave fam a hundred pounds of loud I knew he couldn't sell. Because I needed somewhere to safely stash it. That he sold in less than 48-hours. Then walks in with the ledger two people just died trying to get. I ain't the smartest, but make it make sense." Shaq explained.

"Dig that," Vel said. "Keshaun just walked in behind them. I'll call you back in a second." Vel said ending the call.

****
****

Chapter 7

The FEDS

Agent Whaler parks at the Embassy Suites. He grabs his pen and pad then heads for the entrance of the hotel. As the doors slide open, he is greeted by the front desk.

"I'm visiting," he says walking in discreetly.

"Well, let us know if you plan on staying and have a great day sir!" The clerk replies.

Agent Whaler gets on the elevator with Keshaun, Chris and OOG. The doors close. All four men seemed to be headed to the same floor. There was an awkward silence. Ding! 5th floor the elevator chimed. Keshaun got off first, looking at his phone. Agent Whaler got off next and took a left headed for Sean and Kish's room.

Chris and OOG made a right, they had yet to see the room Desirae had paid for.

Agent Whaler made it to Sean and Kish's room first. He knocked on the door and Sean answered.

"How can I help you?" He asked.

"Investigator Todd Whaler. I believe we spoke over the phone?" he said, while putting his badge away.

"Oh yea. Would you like to step inside? It's been a long week for both of us," Sean answered.

Agent Whaler stepped inside the room.

"Is it safe to say that you are Ms. Mahome?" Agent Whaler asked.

"Yes, call me

Kish," She replied. Agent Whaler nodded.

"I will get down to business. Did you see anything out of the ordinary? Obviously, it was a home invasion. But were they demanding money or looking for anything in particular jewelry, a safe, records?" he asked.

"I don't know. When I came downstairs, they we're busting the ceiling out," Kish replied. If it weren't for the noise, I wouldn't have known they were inside the house," she said.

"When Homicide arrived who did you speak with?" Agent Whaler asked.

"Detective Shambone and Det. Ponder." Kish replied.

"I spoke with Det. Ponder. I should be seeing her soon. Did you know the intruders?" He asked.

"No." Kish responded. "A friend of mine knew them," she said.

"They were Tony Keys' men. The Detectives thought so also." Sean added.

"I don't remember Detective Ponder mentioning that part. Tony Keys" he said, writing in his note pad.

"In the photos I didn't see a getaway car. No third suspect, maybe the driver?" Agent Whaler asked.

"Honestly it happened so quick I never thought to look for anybody else. I called my fiancée and the police immediately after," Kish responded.

"I understand." Agent Whaler said. "Well, that's about all I can think of, but I will

check into this Keys fella and with Det. Shambone and Ponder." Agent Whaler said.

****
****

Chris and OOG were walking down the hallway unaware of Shaq's goon lurking slowly behind them. As they reached the room OOG knocked twice.

"It's me Bae," he said. You could hear the deadbolt unlock then Desirae was standing in the doorway.

"Come on in," she said, turning and walking to the couch and sitting down.

"He took it, but for some reason I feel uneasy." OOG said.

"Man, you cool. Shaq cool, they got what they wanted. You see he didn't trip when we told him it was in the bag," Chris replied.

****
****

Who's Who

Keshaun calls Shaq outside the hotel room.

"Keshaun what's good?" Shaq answered. "Man, Lil-A and Bam got killed by a female." Keshaun said.

Shaq looked at the phone. "A female? How you know that?" Shaq asked.

"The two dudes you said to follow went in the room." Keshaun explained.

"She asked how it went. She fine though hope you ain't gone kill shawty," he said.

"I don't give a fuck about her," Shaq replied. "But Keys wants her brought to him. So, watch her if you can throw her ass in the trunk." Shaq ordered.

****
****

Desirae looks through her purse.

"Bae, do you have a wrap." Desirae asked.

"Nope, I forgot to stop like you asked me." OOG replied.

"Well, let me see the keys I will go to the store. I know you been running all day," she said.

Desirae took the keys, grabbed her purse and walked out the hotel room door.

Agent Whaler was at the elevator when Keshaun and Desirae came around the corner.

The door to the elevator seemed to open up as if commanded.

"Excuse me?" Keshaun said, to Desirae as the doors closed. "I was tryna think of something to say that would make you smile, but for the first time ever yo beauty has left me speechless, he said as Desirae smiled.

Agent Whaler laughed aloud "I've arrested drunks with better pick up lines than that," he said jokingly.

"That's how you got yo wife to say I do? Slapped the cuffs on her then took her to the station?" Keshaun, shot back.

"I was just busting your balls," Agent Whaler said.

"Mind yo damn business," Keshaun said as the elevator chimed 1st floor and the doors slid open.

Desirae exited first, then Keshaun and next Agent Whaler.

Agent Whaler lingered back. He was looking for a reason to arrest Shaq's goon it was something that didn't sit right with him about the guy and he was a smart ass. He quickly brought his attention back to the murder of his confidential informant and the self-defense double homicide. He still watched as Desirae's car pulled out the parking lot.

He noticed that Shaq's goon was following closely behind her. As they drove off in the distance Agent Whaler's thoughts shifted back to his work. He needed to talk to the Detectives.

****
****

Detective Shambone had come in early. His mind swirling with accusations and motives.

The door swung open it was Lilly. "Rough night?" she asked, as she placed donuts and coffee on the desk.

"If were being honest yes, I saw Keys last night. I tried to follow him but a train came between us. So, yeah long night for me." Det. Shambone said.

"Funny," Lilly said. "I saw Keys last night too. I showed him pictures of his men dead at our crime scene, and informed him we were close to busting his ass. That is if someone else didn't bust it first" she said.

Det. Shambone was relieved that Lilly didn't withhold her meeting with Keys. He was worried he may lose his lead now that Keys knew they were on to him.

"Was he surprised when you gave him the pictures?" Detective Shambone asked.

"The motherfucker tried to order me a cranberry cocktail and told me he wasn't worried because dead men didn't talk!" Lilly exclaimed.

"Asshole," Det. Shambone replied. "I thought you were off today?" He asked as his voice softened.

"I am. Thought you might want to know about Keys. Plus, I wanted coffee and donuts thought you might have wanted some too. Well don't work too hard Detective and get some rest tonight. The goal is to retire right?" Lily asked rhetorically. As she grabbed her coffee and headed for the door.

****
****

What's Taking So Long

OOG looks at his watch then asks Chris. "Do you own a firearm?"

"A gun? Yeah, it's at the house." Chris answered, annoyed at the question.

"I pistol whipped a gang member on the corner of Crenshaw once." OOG said.

"In a movie? Chris, asked.

"Yeah, how did you know?" OOG asked.

"Man, I'm about to go home." Chris said even more annoyed.

"Mastering the Arts is real; you can become anything you put your mind too." OOG said enthusiastically.

"Can you catch bullets with yo teeth?" Chris asked, sarcastically.

"What?" OOG asked confused.

"Motherfucka, can you catch bullets with yo teeth?" Chris asked angrily.

"That's impossible." OOG said.

"Then until you can show me how to become superman don't come telling me about no damn arts," Chris said. "I thought I was Micheal Jackson for 26 years. I couldn't shum-on or moonwalk, and my hair fell out when I put the curl kit in it." Chris said.

"Damn, the negativity," OOG said. As he looks at his watch. "A man," OOG says. Desirae been gone for a long time. With a look of concern, he pulls out his phone and calls her twice, but both times it went to voicemail."

****
****

Agent Whaler goes against his gut instincts to follow Shaq's goon as he watched both cars leave the parking lot. After what seemed like an eternity, Agent Whaler pulls out of the hotel parking lot and heads for the gas station. After pulling in he grabs his files. He had known exactly who Tony Key's was. Carlos Ortiz was his confidential informant after all. Hearing his name only confirmed his suspicions that Keys was involved.

As Agent Whaler walked inside, he took a quick glance around the store. He then asked the clerk for $50 on pump #6 and a box of Newport's.

"That'll be $64.40 cash or card?" the clerk asked.

"Cash." Agent Whaler responded handing the clerk exact change. He grabbed his receipt and walked out the store.

Slowing up a bit, he glanced at the car parked in the lot. It looked a lot like the pretty young lady's car from the hotel, but he didn't see her inside the store.

Dismissing it, he began to pump his gas.

After fueling up, he placed the gas pump back into its holder and slid into his

unmarked car and pulled off. He was hoping to catch Det. Ponder and Detective Shambone tonight. He remembered he had an address for Detective Ponder in his files and decided to head there first.

A fifteen- minute drive turned into a 30-minute commute. He was held up by the train that took forever to pass it even stopped on the tracks at one point. Finally, turning on Maple drive. He quickly found the address. To his surprise the rude guy from the hotel was in the backyard with about three other people. But before Agent Whaler could get out the car they were gone.

****
****

"You got your keys? Desirae has mine." OOG asked Chris.

"I gottem," Chris responded. "Where was she going?" Chris asked.

"To the store to get Hemp wraps." OOG answered.

"Come on," Chris said as they headed out the door. OOG was quiet as they sat in the car and he remained silent until he saw his car parked at the gas station.

He and Chris hopped out. Chris ran into the store and OOG opened the car door. The keys were still in the ignition. Her phone was sitting on the arm rest. A tear ran down OOG's cheek. Chris came out of the store and said, "She ain't in there." As he looked into the car, he saw the keys and phone still inside.

"What do we do now?" Chris asked.

"We get ready for war," OOG responded with a look Chris hadn't seen on him before.

****
****

Desirae

Agent Whaler gets out the car, then heads up the driveway to the front door.

"Tie this Bitch up!" Keys yells. The doorbell chimes. Everyone in the basement became quiet.

"Who the fuck is that?" Keyshawn said whispering, rope in hand.

"Go see." Keys whispered and looked at Lillian. "I thought nobody knew about this house?" he asked.

 Agent Whaler rang the doorbell again this time he grabbed the screen door. It was unlocked, so he opened it and knocked directly on the door.

 Keyshawn answered and flung the door open. "Can I help you?" he asked.

"I was looking for Detective Lillian Ponder," Agent Whaler said.

"You got the wrong address. Shawty don't live here." Keyshawn said, as he closed the door.

Agent Whaler was confused as he walked back to his car. "That was definitely the guy from the hotel," he said aloud standing outside his car.

"Who was it?" Keys asked curiously.

"The cop from the hotel," Keshawn answered.

"Lillian!" Keys called out in a muffled voice.

"Who was that?" Lillian asked as she came up the stairs leaving Desirae alone in the basement.

"Shit how we supposed to know he came looking for you. Said, yo whole government name and everything," Keshawn said.

"Look, if he a cop why is he here looking for you? Why his ass ain't go to the station?" Keys asked.

Desirae through all the commotion was never tied up. She quietly and slowly walked up the basement stairs and out the back door. She sprinted out the backyard right past Agent Whaler who had no idea she had ran past him. He had his back turned and was on the phone with GPD. Someone was going to connect him with Det. Shambone right now.

"Hi, I was trying to be connected with Det. Joe Shambone. This is Agent Whaler. Thank you!" he said speaking into his phone.

****
****

OOG and Chris went to Sean's room knocking hard on the door.

"Man, who is it?" Sean said as he flung the door open.

OOG stood there with tears in his eyes. "They got her dawg! I need your help," he said.

"They got who, Desirae? Sean asked sitting on the bed.

"Man Yes!" OOG exclaimed.

"Damn. Tell me what happened." Sean asked.

"We came back from the club and she left to get wraps." OOG said.

"Was anyone following y'all around the hotel or the club?" Sean asked.

"No." OOG replied.

"Wait it was a dude on the elevator," Chris remembered. "I thought he looked familiar," he said.

"Who was it?" Sean asked.

"Chrissean, Keyshawn something like that, but I know I seen him with Keys before," Chris said.

"I won't risk Desirae," Sean said. "Chris, can you set up a meeting with Keys?" Sean asked.

"I should be able to, Shaq been pretty cool." Chris answered.

"Cool, have him meet you at the bar we need a crowd," Sean said as he stood up.

"I'm going with you," OOG said.

"Nah man. You stay here in case Desirae shows up. We could be jumping the gun," Sean replied.

"What time you wanna meet?" Chris asked.

"Around 8 o'clock that'll give me time to figure something out," Sean said. "Don't call from the hotel, call from the bar have him meet you there." Sean said as he walked out the door.

****
****

Chapter 8

All Or Nothing

Detective Shambone was at his desk when the call came in.

"Call on #2 Detective," the desk clerk said as she closed the door.

"Det. Shambone speaking," he answered.

"Detective I'm Agent Whaler investigating the death of my C.I. Carlos Ortiz. I must say I'm usually laid back, reserved if you get where I'm coming from." Agent Whaler said.

"Lay it on me," Det. Shambone replied. "What seems to be the problem?" he asked.

"I have a conflict of interest. I spoke with a Sean Flattery and Kish Mahome. They seem to think Tony Keys is behind their case," he explained.

"The perps were affiliated with Keys," Det. Shambone said.

"Well Detective Ponder failed to mention that when we spoke a couple of days ago," Agent Whaler responded.

"Lilly is pretty good about details Agent Whaler," Det. Shambone said.

"Which brings me to my next dilemma," Agent Whaler said. "I went by the address I have for Det. Ponder and there were some strange coincidences and characters at the address," Agent Whaler explained.

"Agent Whaler, Lilly is off the next four days," Det. Shambone said. "If you like I can meet you at the address you have and we can put to bed any suspicions you may have," Detective Shambone offered.

"That sounds reasonable give me an hour. I have some things to look into." Agent Whaler responded.

****
****

With Sean gone OOG paced back and forth.

"How can I just wait in a room while God only knows what is happening to Desirae," he said aloud. OOG had the car keys and phone. He had thought about calling the police, but what if they were in on it. Besides he had taken pictures of the ledger. If they found out about that, everyone would be dead for sure.

The door handle started to jiggle. OOG opened the door to his surprise it was Desirae. She burst into tears as she fell into his arms.

"I thought I would never see you again," she said crying.

"Bae! What happened?" OOG asked. "This guy followed me from the hotel. He said I was leaking gas. When I pulled into the gas station to check he pulled a gun out and forced me in his car. He took me to a house it was other people there waiting.

They took me down in the basement but someone came to the door. I think it was a cop because everyone was all nervous and weren't paying me any attention. They didn't tie me up. So, while they were all scared trying to see who the man was I snuck out and ran as fast as I could," she explained.

"Do you know who they were?" OOG asked.

"No." Desirae said. "They didn't say any names. It was so quiet when the cop came to the door I just ran.

"I gotta call Sean, they on the way to meet Keys," OOG said.

****

****

What Can Will

Sean couldn't think straight. He had given Chris all the money he had with him. It would have taken him an hour to drive to get the money. Then to meet Chris, so he waited. It may be the only leverage they have. If Shaq would set up the meeting, Sean was willing to get the money for Desirae.

If it was Keys' money, he would have to give him all that he had and they may never see Sean or Desirae again. As he pulled up, Sean saw Chris's car parked. Sean parked and got out. He couldn't tell if he was nervous but something didn't feel right. Deep breath he told himself exhaling as he opened the door. It was always crowded.

Sean scanned the room and saw Shaq at the bar, but Chris wasn't with him. Not thinking of the danger, Sean walked over and tapped Shaq on the shoulder.

"Where's Chris?" Sean asked.

Shaq turned toward him "Big Money," he said with a smile. "You just missed him," then spun around as if they weren't having a conversation.

Talking to the guy next to him Sean asked, "Is this Keys?"

The look he gave Sean only confirmed his suspicions. Sean's phone rang, thinking it was Chris, he answered it.

"Hello!" Sean said.

"Get out of there Desirae is here with me right now." OOG said.

It was too late, Sean hung up the phone without saying a word.

Shaq spun around and was now standing. "Sit down," Shaq demanded."

It was in that moment he knew he fucked up. Sean was shook as he sat down.

"You know most people don't like to meet with me," Keys said looking Sean in the eye. "Because that means they gone die," he said with malice.

"You're a businessman, right?" Sean asked, nervously.

"What could you possibly have that would make me want to do business with you?" Keys questioned.

"The house. I know who owns it, you could buy it," Sean said.

"Fuck that house," Keys responded. "All I wanted was the ledger which I have now. So, if you know about the house you know about the ledger." Keys said.

"What ledger?" Sean asked, caught off guard.

"I tell you what," Keys said as he grabbed a napkin off the bar. "A million dollars. Meet me at this address at 9 o'clock or you and everybody you love gone die," he said as he stood up and walked out the bar. Shaq followed closely behind him.

Sean walked out of the bar behind Keys and Shaq. Sean was watching and scanning the parking lot. Chris' car was still parked in the same spot. Sean walked over but it was hard to see inside with the tent on the windows. As he reached the driver's side door, he grabbed the handle and the door popped open. Chris fell out hitting the ground.

"CHRIS," Sean yelled. He tried lifting Chris' head up. Sean could see what looked like bruising around Chris' neck. He was strangled.

Sean layed him on the ground and felt for a pulse, he was cold and obviously dead.

He dialed 911. The operator answered the phone "Police, Fire or EMS?" she said.

"I'm in Maple, Heights. I need an ambulance at the Remedy night club. HURRY! There's a man unresponsive in the parking lot.

My Name. Sean Flattery. HURRY PLEASE!" Sean shouted into his phone. He couldn't wait for the ambulance or the cops. Sean stayed until he heard the sirens in the distance.

What did I do? Sean thought as he drove doing 45 mph in a 25 mile an hour zone. Easing off the gas pedal Sean checked the address 4260 Maple Drive. Sean was in deep thought. Thinking to himself that Keys was going to kill him regardless. But if he ran, Keys would come after everyone Sean loved Kish, OOG, shit they already kidnapped Desirae. Before he knew it, he was doing 45 again.

His next move was to get the money safely. Two hours. Sean had two hours. Keys would pay for what they did to Chris. Even if it meant losing his life, and dying wasn't an option. Sean's phone was ringing and it didn't register right away. He looked down and saw the screen lit up. He answered, "Hello."

"Man, you gotta call somebody. Let us know you're okay," OOG said angrily.

"They killed Chris." Sean said solemnly. "And they want a million dollars or they going to kill us too" He explained.

"What! Damn, man not Chris! That's what Keys said?" OOG asked.

"Meet him tonight with the money. Sean repeated what happened verbatim.

"Where?" OOG asked I'm coming with you."

"Nah, I got Chris killed and Kish had to kill 2 people. It's too much death," Sean said.

"You go alone and give him the money. You know he gone kill you." OOG said.

"I know, but I got us into this I gotta get us out. Let me think, I'll call you later." Sean said, hanging up the phone.

Sean drove to the spot to get the money for the second time today, and the bag just keeps getting bigger. There was no way he was getting out of here without answering some questions. He walked in and his mother was playing Pastor Mike Junior's song "So Good." When she played that song, it meant she was in a good mood.

"In the kitchen cooking," Sean said with a smile.

"Hey baby," Sean's mom said. "This the most I done seen you in one day," she said.

"Yeah, getting this money together for this building I bought," Sean said.

"Sean, I can smell bull junk a mile away. You come in here looking like yo dog done died, and don't think I don't know about all that money in yo closet," his mother informed him.

"You been in my room? Sean asked shaking his head. "Ma, look you can't tell nobody. They killed… You just can't say nothing," he warned.

"So, what you gone pay to have somebody else killed? Revenge is mine says The Lord. What you wanna do is nothing in comparison to what God can do son. Is that what you want revenge?" Sean's mother asked.

"I just wanna make sure no one else is hurt," Sean said frankly.

Sean loaded the million dollars into the duffle bag and walked out. If she knew, it didn't make sense to try and hide it. Sean was starting to not give a fuck about what happened next and he didn't like the feeling. As he sat in the truck, Sean pulled his wallet out and the Detective's card fell out. Sean wasn't sure who needed to die. But if Keys killed Chris, he owed it to him to make it right.

Sean dialed the number and pressed the call button.

Detective Shambone answered the phone as he walked into the hospital.

"Detective Shambone speaking," he said.

"Detective, this is Sean Flattery my fiancée shot the two intruders," Sean said unsure he'd remember.

"E.84th. How can I help you," Det. Shambone said.

"My friend was murdered at the bar about an hour ago," Sean said.

"That was your friend?" Det. Shambone asked. "I'm at the hospital now. Look son whatever you're into I can help," he said.

"It may be too late for me. I'm going to meet Keys now." Sean said.

"That's not a good idea. Where are you meeting him?" Detective Shambone asked.

"Maple Drive. He killed my friend, if I die just know he killed me too." Sean said, and hung up the phone.

****

****

"I'm Detective Shambone," he said while simultaneously flashing the nurse his badge.

"D.O.A. victim came in from Garfield, Heights," he said as he walked up to the information desk. "He's in with the examiner. Room #2 second door on the left." The nurse at the information desk said.

Detective Shambone thanked the nurse as he walked into the examination room. A white sheet was covering the body. The medical examiner hadn't started the autopsy. He turned and greeted Detective Shambone.

"I can tell you this," he said. as he walked to where Chris' head lay. "Strangulation was the cause of death. Whoever did this stood or sat behind the victim. Poor guy lost 8 fingernails. That means he fought like hell trying to get whatever was used from around his neck," the medical examiner said as he explained his theory.

Detective Shambone looked on as he listened. He needed to call Tosha, see if she had heard anything.

He pulled out his phone. It was a quarter till 8 when his phone lit up. It was Agent Whaler. He walked out of the examination room and answered the phone.

"Hello, Agent Whaler," he said.

"Detective I know I'm late, but I still wanna check out this Keys fella. This is the same guy I saw today. Something strange is going down. There is a lot of traffic in and out at this house. Someone is going in as we speak," Agent Whaler said.

"What's the address?" Detective Shambone asked.

"4260 Maple Drive." Agent Whaler replied.

"Did you say Maple Drive?" Detective Shambone asked.

"Yes 4260," Agent Whaler repeated.

"Wait for me," Detective Shambone said. "I should be there in about 15 minutes,

don't get out or try to pursue Keys. I believe he had a young man murdered tonight. I'm leaving the hospital now," he informed the Agent.

Detective Shambone began walking toward the exit before jogging to his car.

****
****

CHAPTER 9

It Ends Here

Once Sean pulled up at Keys' place, he called Kish to let her know he made it and that he loved her. Sean thought about taking the money inside, but that was the only bargaining chip that he had. Sean hand was shaking when he opened the car door to get out. Scanning the area gave no clue to what was going to happen next. It was dark and hotter than usual.

Maybe it was the anxiety he thought as he walked up to the front door. There was a sign "use back door" on it. He felt even worse not knowing who was waiting on him up the driveway or at the back door.

Keys was standing silently at the back door smoking a cigarette.

"You're early, I like early," Keys said. Blowing smoke out his nose.

Keys turned and went inside the house. Sean walked in behind him. They walked through the kitchen then into the living room. Keys turned and looked down at Sean's hands and asked, "Where's the money?"

"It's safe," Sean said. "How do I know you won't kill me when you have it?" Sean asked.

If looks could kill, Sean would be dead. Keys' eyes were like nothing Sean had ever seen before.

Keys said "If I don't get it, I'm going to kill you anyway."

"We found the ledger," Sean said. "We didn't even open it," he said.

When Detective Ponder came in, she asked, "What ledger?" looking at Keys.

"To ensure my safety, that ledger," Keys said.

****
****
■■■

Detective Shambone turned left on Maple Drive, there were cars lined up and down the street. He didn't know what kind of car Agent Whaler drove and it was dark. He stopped, parked and got out of his car. He flashed the flashlight standing in front of 4268. He began to walk down the street flashing the light again 4260 this was it.

He didn't see anything as he walked up the driveway. He saw what looked like shoes, as he came closer it was a body of a white male. This had to be Agent Whaler. Detective Shambone rolled him over checking for a pulse, gunshots or stab wounds, but there were none. He was just knocked unconscious.

Detective Shambone called for an ambulance. He began to hear voices coming

from the house, a male voice. "We found the ledger and gave it back. We never even opened it." The male voice explained.

"What ledger?" a female voice responded.

"To ensure my safety, that ledger," another male voice yelled.

Detective Shambone was standing at the back door that stood wide open. He slowly walked into the house, careful not to make a sound as he walked through the kitchen.

The female voice said "There were rumors of something like this."

As Detective Shambone positioned himself to get a line of sight, he could see the woman it was Lilly. Agent Whaler was right. Before he could say a word Detective Ponder placed the gun to Keys' head and pulled the trigger.

"Freeze," Detective Shambone yelled pointing the gun at Lilly as Tony Keys' body fell to the floor.

"Detective Ponder place the gun on the floor," Det. Shambone yelled.

 Lilly looked at Sean and said "today is your lucky day." Then looking at Detective Shambone Lilly said "Out of all the people you show up" still clutching her gun.

"Put the gun down Detective. Look Keys can be explained, but what does Flattery have to do with this?" Det. Shambone asked.

Detective Ponder looked at Detective Shambone "That ledger can't leave this room with anyone, but me." She said.

"That's what this is about a ledger? What about your career? Your freedom?" he asked.

Lilly was stoned faced still clutching her service pistol. "Everything I did was for my freedom. I was never a cop; my entire mission was that ledger. I never truly knew if he had it, we only heard about it," she said. Turning toward Detective Shambone raising her weapon three shots echoed.

 Lilly fell backward firing a single shot into the ceiling. Detective Shambone's head dropped in disappointment. Five years of working alongside Detective Ponder. Who knew it would come to this.

You could hear the sirens in the distance.

Detective Shambone looked at Sean, "God didn't want you to go not like this, not like this," he said as he turned and walked through the kitchen and out the back door. Sean followed behind him as fire trucks and ambulances pulled up to the scene.

****
****

A week later Sean, Kish, OOG and Desirae went to Chris' funeral. Sean had paid for everything; it was the least he could do. After leaving the cemetery Sean stopped at the gas station to fill up. While inside a man in his mid-twenties to early thirties, in tip top shape walked over to Sean.

He asked, "If someone had millions of dollars that didn't belong to him how would you go about getting it back?"

Sean's life flashed before his eyes and he began to stutter. The man pointed to his ear.

"My bag Bruh I'm on the phone." he said. As he began to fill his slushy cup.

To be continued……..

Book 2

The Ledger

Detective Shambone cleared the last picture off his desk, before heading down to evidence to see Property Clerk Whirley. Whirley was one of the new recruits Det. Shambone had taken a liking too. Plus, he gave Shambone his parlay picks which turned out to be winners. So, Det. Shambone wanted his advice on this Sunday's games.

Everyone said their goodbye's and congratulated the Detective as he walked down the hall. He then used his badge to swipe in to the basement. Once at evidence he

stood at the locked gate. No one was present so, he rang the bell once, twice then a young Hispanic officer appeared. Collins his name tag read.

Detective Shambone asked "Where's Whirley? I thought he was on shift today?"

"Had an emergency I'm covering," the officer replied smiling.

Det. Shambone smiled, "No worries. I'll call him later," he said.

Det. Shambone walked off and up the stairs back to the main lobby to leave when Property Clerk Whirley walked in.

"Whirley, Det. Shambone said. Everything, okay?"

"Mendoza was having an issue with a guy going into booking," Property Clerk Whirley responded.

"But I've never seen Mendoza before, I thought we were the new recruits?" he asked.

Det. Shambone's eyes grew wide, it was at that moment he realized they had been infiltrated. With no hesitation he turned and ran back to the basement with Whirley on his heels. They swiped in and went straight to the evidence lockers.

The gate was open with no one inside. Det. Shambone only knew of one thing in evidence worth breaking in for. He walked around to the isle it was filed in. The box lay on the floor empty.

"Lock this department down now!" he yelled. "Radio the Chief and someone get me an ID on officer Collins." The Detective ordered.

****
****

Book 2: The Ledger Coming Soon!